Ready Steady Read!

LEVEL 4

D

C

su

A
ar
w

A
sk
w

Th
m

As   ung
re   y
re   ding
to

Pr

Lecturer in Literacy and Children's Books

How to use this series

The **Ready, Steady, Read!** series has 4 levels.
The facing page shows what you can expect to find
in the books at each level.

As your child's confidence grows, they can progress
to books from the higher levels. These will keep them
engaged and encourage new reading skills.

The levels are only meant as guides; together, you and
your child can pick the book that will be just right.

Here are some handy tips for helping children who are
ready for reading!

Give them choice – Letting children pick a book
(from the level that's right for them) makes them
feel involved.

Talk about it – Discussing the story and the
pictures helps children engage with the book.

Read it again – Repetition of favourite stories
reinforces learning.

Cheer them on! – Praise and encouragement
builds a child's confidence and the belief in their
growing ability.

LEVEL 1 — For first readers

* short, straightforward sentences
* basic, fun vocabulary
* simple, easy-to-follow stories of up to 100 words
* large print and easy-to-read design

LEVEL 2 — For developing readers

* longer sentences
* simple vocabulary, introducing new words
* longer stories of up to 200 words
* bold design, to capture readers' interest

LEVEL 3 — For more confident readers

* longer sentences with varied structure
* wider vocabulary
* high-interest stories of up to 300 words
* smaller print for experienced readers

LEVEL 4 — For able readers

* longer sentences with complex structure
* rich, exciting vocabulary
* complex stories of up to 400 words
* emphasis on text more than illustrations

Make Reading Fun!

Once you have read the story, you will find some amazing activities at the back of the book! There are Excellent Exercises for you to complete, plus a super Picture Dictionary.

But first it is time for the story . . .

Ready?
Steady?
Let's read!

A H Benjamin   John Bendall-Brunello

Mouse, Mole
and the
Falling Star

LITTLE TIGER PRESS
London

Mole and Mouse were best friends.

They always helped each other.

"I'm lucky to have you," Mole would say.

"I'm lucky to have *you!*" Mouse would reply.

One evening, Mouse said to Mole,
"You know, a fallen star can make
your wishes come true."

"Wow!" said Mole. "Imagine that!"

Just then, a shooting star
zipped across the sky.

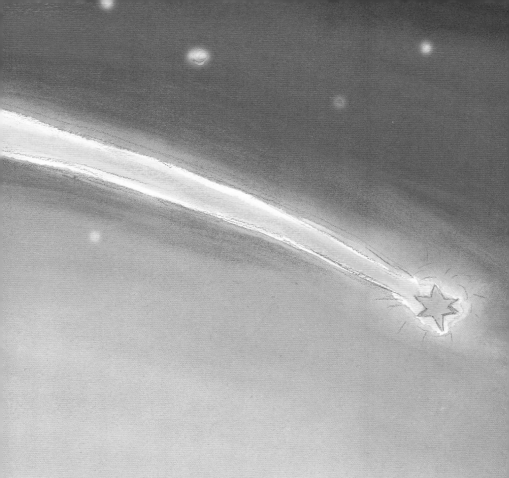

"It's a fallen star," gasped Mole.
   "I'm going to find it!" cried Mouse.

"It's my star!" called Mole.
"I saw it first."
   "I saw it first!" shouted
Mouse. "It's *my* star!"

Mole and Mouse started
searching for the fallen star.

"I'll look for it in the woods tomorrow,"
thought Mouse.

Mole thought the same.

But they did not tell each other
what they were thinking.

And they both went home without
even saying goodnight.

The next day, Mole and Mouse both
sneaked out to the woods to look for
the fallen star.

Mole found a patch of burned grass.
"This must be where the star fell,"
he thought.
"Mouse must
have taken it."

A little later, Mouse found the same
patch of grass.
"The star has
gone!" he cried.
"I bet Mole has it!"

Mole and Mouse were feeling very angry.

"You stole my star!" they yelled at each other.

Later, Mole sneaked into Mouse's house
to find the star . . .

And Mouse looked through
Mole's window to see
where Mole had
hidden it.

But neither
found the
fallen star.

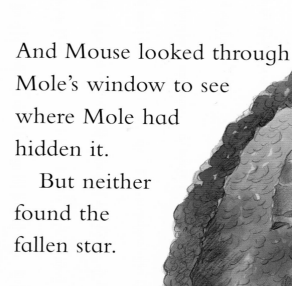

The days rolled by and Mole and
Mouse grew sad and lonely.
  "All I want is my friend back,"
thought Mouse.

"I wish Mouse were still my friend,"
thought Mole.

Then one day, Mouse spotted a golden leaf, swirling and twirling in the air.

"It's the fallen star!" cried Mouse. "I'll catch it for Mole."

"It's Mouse's star," thought Mole. "I'll help him catch it."

But the leaf was already high in the sky, glimmering in the sunshine. It swayed this way and that, as if waving goodbye, and then vanished altogether.

"We don't need a star," said Mouse.
"We have each other."
　　"We do," agreed Mole.

Then they lay on top of the hill with their arms and legs stretched out. And they looked just like two furry stars!

The Biggest Baddest Wolf

Harum Scarum is the biggest, baddest, hairiest, scariest wolf in the city. And he loves to frighten people! But when he loses his teddy, he doesn't seem so scary after all . . .

Meggie Moon

Digger and Tiger spend all their time in the Yard. It's full of junk and it's their place. Then one day someone arrives, wanting to play . . .

The Nutty Nut Chase

The animals are having a race! And the winner gets to eat a delicious, brown nut. But the race does not go as planned. And the nut seems to have a life of its own!

Robot Dog

Scrap the Robot Dog has a dent on his ear. So he is sent to the junkyard, with the other rejected toys. Will he ever find an owner?

In memory of my father and mother — A H B
To all my friends and my dearest wife, Tiziana — J B

LITTLE TIGER PRESS, 1 The Coda Centre, 189 Munster Road, London SW6 6AW
First published in Great Britain 2002
This edition published 2013
Text copyright © A H Benjamin 2002, 2013
Illustrations copyright © John Bendall-Brunello 2002, 2013
All rights reserved
Printed in China
978-1-84895-681-0
LTP/1800/0601/0413
2 4 6 8 10 9 7 5 3 1

Books in the Series

LEVEL 1 – For first readers

Can't You Sleep, Dotty?

Fred

My Turn!

Rosie's Special Surprise

What Bear Likes Best!

LEVEL 2 – For developing readers

Hopping Mad!

Newton

Ouch!

Where There's a Bear, There's Trouble!

The Wish Cat

LEVEL 3 – For more confident readers

Lazy Ozzie

Little Mouse and the Big Red Apple

Nobody Laughs at a Lion!

Ridiculous!

Who's Been Eating My Porridge?

LEVEL 4 – For able readers

The Biggest Baddest Wolf

Meggie Moon

Mouse, Mole and the Falling Star

The Nutty Nut Chase

Robot Dog